Text: Jörg Steiner / Pictures: Jörg Müller

# Rabbit Island

Translation by
Ann Conrad Lammers

## The BERGH Publishing Group, Inc.
New York – Stockholm – Zürich

JÖRG MÜLLER, born in 1942 in Lausanne, is active as a graphic artist and illustrator in France as well as in his native Switzerland. His picture portfolio, *The Changing Countryside*, won the German Young People's Books Award in 1973, and it and his second portfolio, *The Changing City*, were voted Notable Children's Books of 1977 by the American Library Association.

JÖRG STEINER, born in 1930, lives and works as a teacher and writer in Biel, Switzerland. He is the winner of the international Charles Veillon Prize. His books, novels, stories, and poems have been translated into many languages. *Rabbit Island* is the second picture book he has produced in collaboration with the illustrator Jörg Müller.

Illustrations and German language text copyright © 1977 by Verlag Sauerländer, Aarau (Switzerland)

Originally published by Verlag Sauerländer AG, Aarau, Switzerland, under the title of *Die Kanincheninsel*

First American edition 1978
Printed in Germany

Second American edition 1985
Printed in Singapore

Library of Congress Cataloging in Publication Data
Steiner, Jörg.
Rabbit Island.

Translation of Die Kanincheninsel.
SUMMARY: The adventures of two rabbits who escape from the rabbit factory.
[1. Rabbits—Fiction] I. Müller, Jörg.
II. Title.
PZ7.S8262Rab 1978   [E]   78-1512

ISBN 0-930267-00-1

Factories that produce chocolate are chocolate factories. Factories that make guns are gun factories. But the factory in this story is a rabbit factory. It has no chimney and makes very little noise.

Other factories have machines, but the rabbit factory just has conveyor belts rolling through it, carrying small pellets of rabbit food. Behind the belts sit hundreds of rabbits in narrow cages eating whatever comes along because they have nothing else to do. In this way they quickly grow fat. When they get fat enough, they will be slaughtered, but they don't know that. They also don't know whether it is summer or winter, day or night, for the factory has no windows, only gentle artificial light.

One morning a truck stopped in front of the factory, as it did every day. Some men took boxes from it and carried them into the factory, where the conveyer belts were.

A big gray rabbit, who had been living in the factory for a long time, watched the men open the boxes.

"Now, now, who's this trembling so hard?" he asked a little brown rabbit who had just been taken from the first box. But the little brown rabbit only pressed himself fearfully into the farthest corner of the cage.

"Some rabbits have long ears and some have short ones," said Big Gray. "Some rabbits have red eyes and some have black ones. If there's anything you want to know, you can just ask me. I've been living here a long time—a long, long time."

"I'm scared," whispered Little Brown. "I'm awfully scared."

"We're all happy here," said Big Gray. "You don't have to be afraid. The men are always bringing in boxes with small skinny rabbits, and they're always filling up boxes with big fat rabbits and taking them away. That's how life is; you can't change it."

"What happens to the big rabbits that get taken away?" asked Little Brown.

"Nobody knows, exactly," said Big Gray. "None of them has ever come back. But I'm told they're taken to a much better place. They say enormous white rabbits live there."

"As big as you?" asked Little Brown.

"Of course! Much bigger," said Big Gray. "So big, you can't imagine it. They say the big white rabbits keep watch over all the other ones. The White Watch Rabbits protect the good rabbits, and they skin the bad ones alive. If you're careful not to do anything bad, you can live there happily for ever and ever."

Little Brown thought about the farm where he had lived before the men had come along in a truck and taken him away. "Do beets grow there, too?" he asked. "And does the sun shine in the daytime and the moon at night?"

Big Gray blinked. He had long since forgotten what beets were, living in the factory, but he didn't want to admit that to Little Brown. "Beets and sun and moon," he said, and wrinkled his nose. "Of course, they have those, too."

"Then the land of the White Watch Rabbits is exactly like my farm," said Little Brown, "where we hunt for our own food. Do you remember grass and clover, and leaves and roots and bark?"

"Of course I remember." Big Gray lied.

"There must be trees there," said Little Brown, "and soft earth to dig holes and burrows and tunnels in."

"Of course there are," said Big Gray, who didn't know any more what a tree was, or sand, or soft earth. "Everybody knows that. Really, this talk is beginning to bore me."

"I don't want to bore you," said Little Brown. "I just wish we could see for ourselves how it looks there and not have to wait until the men take us there in a box."

"That's a pretty good idea," said Big Gray, and he looked around cautiously. "For a long time, in fact, I've been working on a plan, and I know how we might get out of here. Of course, I'm pretty big and strong, and the men will probably be coming to get me soon."

"But what will become of *me*, then?" asked Little Brown. "How will I get along without a friend and all alone?"

"I've got a plan, remember?" said Big Gray. "I can't do it by myself, but we can do it together."

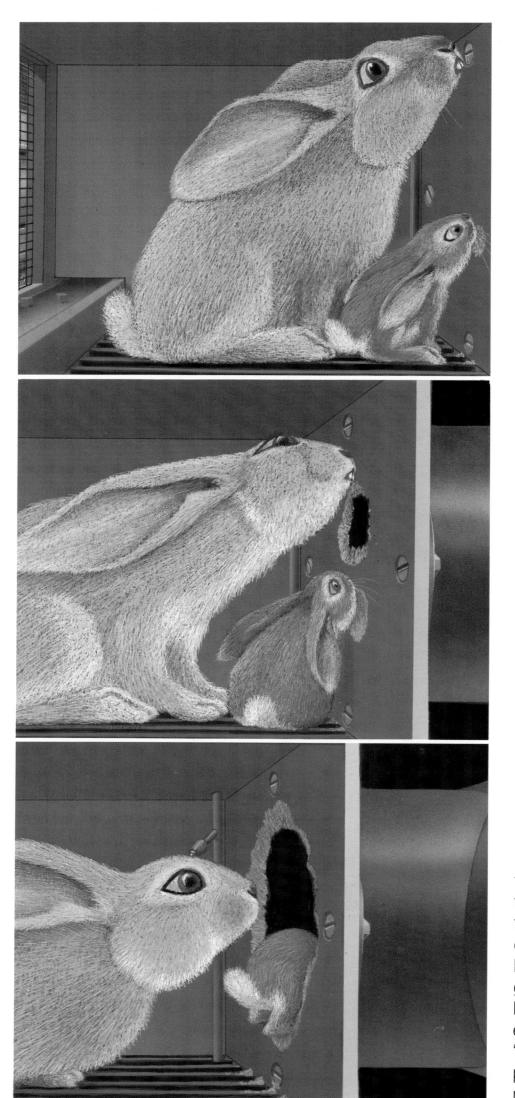

Big Gray had never really thought of trying to run away. He had forgotten that flowers bloomed outside and that there were such things as rain and clouds and snow. He had lived too long in the factory. But now he began gnawing busily, and Little Brown helped him. When the hole was big enough, Little Brown slipped through. "Now if only I don't get stuck," whispered Big Gray as Little Brown hurried on ahead.

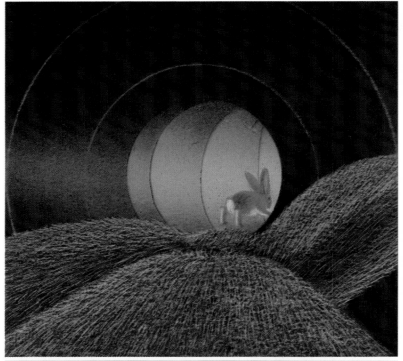

They ran through the air duct until they came to a round opening in the outer wall.

"Big Gray, we made it," whispered Little Brown. "We're free!"

The two sat there for a long time, sniffing the air. The night was summery and warm. Close by, a cricket chirped.

"It smells funny," whispered Big Gray finally.

"It smells of hay," said Little Brown.

"Of course," said Big Gray, although he didn't know any more what hay was.

The two rabbits hopped contentedly through the dewy grass. When Big Gray saw Little Brown pricking up his ears, he did the same. And so, with their ears pointed high, they came to a stream.

"Look at that," said Big Gray. "They're sending us food on a belt, just like at home."

"That's not a belt, I don't think," said Little Brown. "I think it's water in a stream."

"But it flows along, and it rustles," said Big Gray.

"Water can flow, too," said Little Brown.

"Of course," said Big Gray. "Everybody knows that. How do we get across? That's the question."

They hopped along the bank by the stream. Sometimes Little Brown stopped and nibbled on a leaf. Finally Big Gray stood up on his hind legs and looked around.

"Over there is another stream," he said. "But it's a lot wider, and it doesn't seem to be flowing."
"That's no stream," said Little Brown. "That's a road, and I'm scared of roads."
Big Gray didn't know why they ought to be scared of roads. "Let me go first then," he said, and in great leaps the two rabbits jumped across the road—Big Gray in front, Little Brown following.

On the other side, the earth was soft and sandy. Again there was a rustling sound in the air, not like the sound of the stream, but dryer and sharper. It was the wind, rustling in the reeds.

"I'm awfully tired," said Little Brown, who was still hopping along behind Big Gray. "Don't you think we ought to rest a little?"

Big Gray, whose paws were hurting terribly, looked around. "Of course, I could go on for a long time yet," he said, "but I wouldn't object to having a short rest."

So the two lay down in the dry grass, exhausted, and soon fell fast asleep—Little Brown because he was so small, Big Gray because he had forgotten how to run and jump.

They awoke in bright morning light. The sun was blinding. Silvery, shimmering fish darted out of the water.

"My stomach is growling," said Big Gray. "Didn't you say something about beets?"

"Yes," said Little Brown with his cheeks already full. "Only I don't know what a beet field looks like. But you should try these dandelions, or the clover over there!"

They hopped about. Big Gray sniffed cautiously at a leaf.

"I've never eaten food like this," he said sadly—for he'd also forgotten how good clover and dandelion taste. "Actually, I'm not really hungry yet."

Suddenly the reeds behind them parted, and a swan darted at them with its long white neck. Frightened to death, the two rabbits raced away.

"That's one of the White Watch Rabbits!" panted Big Gray as he ran. "He wants to skin us alive because we ran away from home."

Exhausted, the two rabbits cowered in the shade of a tree.

"Anyway, it's gone," said Little Brown, still gasping for breath. "Do you really think it was one of the White Watch Rabbits?"

"What else could it have been?" asked Big Gray.

"It didn't *look* like a rabbit," said Little Brown. "And it came through the water."

"The White Watch Rabbits can swim, too," said Big Gray. "Swim and fly and do absolutely anything."

Little Brown thought this over for a long time. "Well, we don't want to fight about it," he said at last. "White Watch Rabbit or not, we should get to work. Once we have a burrow, we're safe. Nobody can get at us there, and the sunlight won't be so blinding."

With that, he jumped to his feet and began to dig. Now and then he glanced over at Big Gray. What am I going to do with him? he thought. Big Gray is unhappy. He was expecting the world to be different, I guess. "Come on, Big Gray," he called. "Come and help me with the digging! You're so much stronger than I am."

But Big Gray didn't dare come out of the shadow. "My head aches," he moaned. "The White Watch Rabbits are after us. I can't find my kind of food anywhere, and I don't know *how* to dig a burrow. I wish I could go home. It's nicer there than anywhere."

"I didn't like it there at all," said Little Brown. "And we never did find out what happens to the big fat rabbits when they take them away. Anyhow, none of them are here. Do you think they all live in another country?"

Big Gray crept still deeper into the shadow of the tree. From time to time a shudder ran through his body. Little Brown looked at his friend in alarm. "Why aren't you talking any more?" he asked. "Big Gray, what's the matter?"

But Big Gray didn't answer.

Then Little Brown knew that something had to be done. "Big Gray," he said firmly, "if you like, I'll take you home. I know the way by now, and my burrow will be waiting here when I come back."

Big Gray lay as if he were dead, but gradually he stopped trembling. "Would you really go with me?" he asked finally, without raising his head.

"Of course," said Little Brown. "We're friends, aren't we?"

"I'll never forget you for helping me," said Big Gray. "Never, as long as I live."

Little Brown slipped quickly, one more time, into his unfinished burrow; then the two of them started off together.

The midday sun shone through the treetops. Not a breath of wind stirred in the reeds. The air shimmered in the June heat. Beside the water stood a man, fishing. His dog lay next to him, twitching his legs as he slept.

When the fisherman noticed the two rabbits, he whistled through his teeth. "There you lie, dreaming about hunting," he said softly to his dog, "while right under your nose the fattest wild rabbits are hopping by."

The man had often heard of wild rabbits, but until now he'd never seen one. They behave just like ordinary tame rabbits, he thought. The only difference is that tame rabbits don't run around loose; they belong to somebody.

Carefully he laid down his fishing rod. Then he crouched down and waited. He almost caught Little Brown, who hadn't seen him. Only a mighty jump saved Little Brown from the man's strong hands. Growling, the dog sprang up.

And now they were running, Big Gray and Little Brown, really running for their lives.

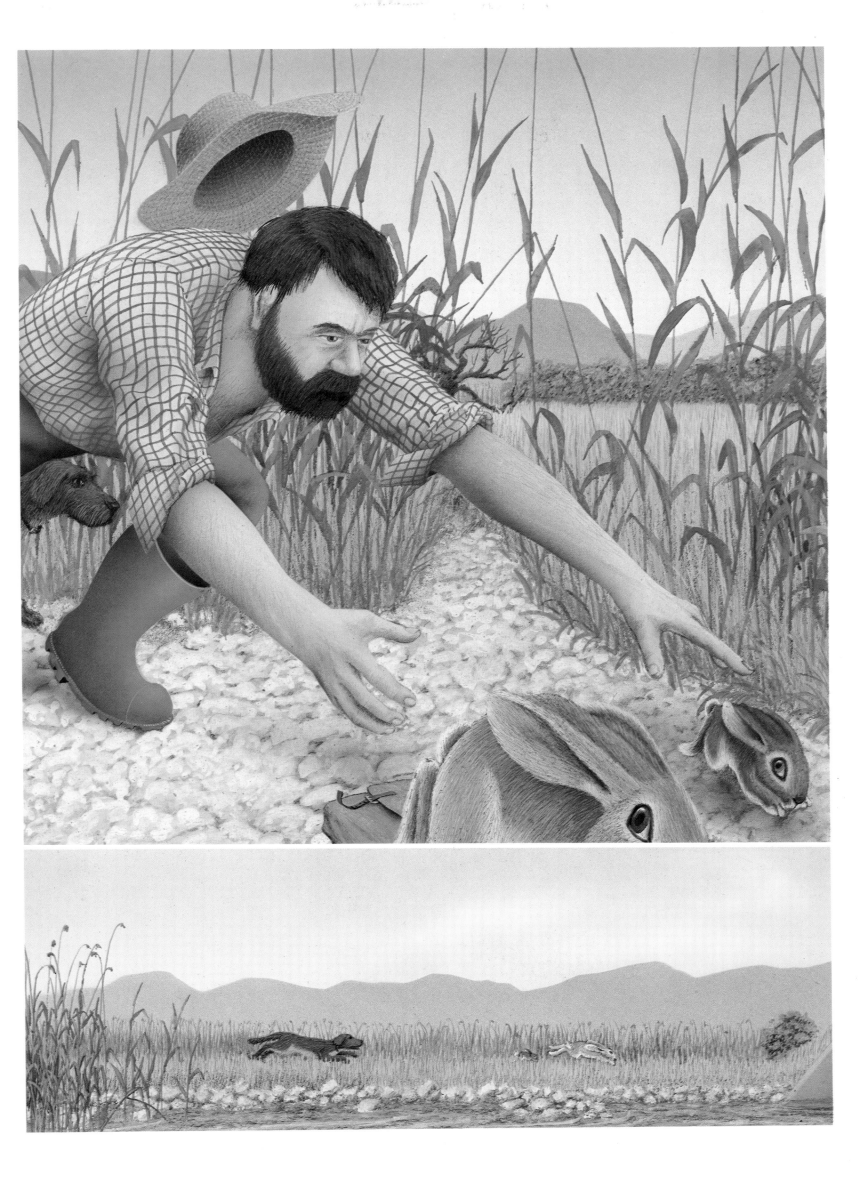

They weren't trying to hide any more. They raced back along the same path they had taken the night before. The dog chased them as far as the road and then stopped. Only now did he start to bark, and his fur stood on end—but he didn't dare to cross the road.

Near the stream, the rabbits dove into the tall grass. They lay there until evening.

Big Gray got his voice back first. "Little Brown," he asked softly, "are you still alive?"

"I think so," said Little Brown.

"We're almost home," said Big Gray. "Nothing more can happen to us now. We escaped together, and now we're going home together."

Little Brown shook his head sadly. "Big Gray," he said, "you know I can't go with you."

"You could if only you wanted to," said Big Gray. "Aren't you afraid of the White Watch Rabbits?"

"Yes, I'm afraid," answered Little Brown. "I'm afraid of the road, and I'm afraid of men and dogs that try to catch me."

"You're very brave," said Big Gray. "And you know your way around in the world better than I do. I've forgotten too much."

"Over there I can already see the lights of the building," said Little Brown. "I'll go that far with you. Then we have to say good-bye."

In silence the two hopped slowly along beside the hedge, up to the building with the gentle artificial light.

But the closer they came, the stranger everything looked.

"That's not our building," whispered Little Brown.

"But it looks a lot like it," said Big Gray, and he started trembling again.

"Don't you worry," said Little Brown. "We'll find our way."

And they did.

Even before the moon rose, the two of them slipped under the fence.

It smelled of hay, and a cricket was chirping nearby.

"I can't stay here very long," said Little Brown. "It's better if I get on my way quickly."

"You're probably right," whispered Big Gray. "Don't forget me, out there in your burrow. Oh, what will I do without you?"

"You'll find a new friend," said Little Brown. "I'm sure of that."

"Not one like you," said Big Gray. But Little Brown didn't hear him. He was already standing by the fence.

"Good luck, Little Brown," called Big Gray. "Good luck!"